The Muse

A short novel by

Paul Riedel

www.paul-riedel.de

©Paul Riedel, Munich 2016

Printed in Germany

Cover: © Paul Riedel, Munich 2016

Lectorate: Tristan Auer, Austria 2019

First German edition 2016

Second German edition 2018

First English Edition 2019

Bibliographic information of the German national library:
The German national library registered this publication
in the German national bibliography, detailed
bibliographic data are available online at www.dnb.de.

© 2019 Paul Riedel

Production and publisher

BoD- Books on Demand, Norderstedt

ISBN: 978-3-7504-0055-9

Paul Riedel

Born on 27 May 1960 in the Brazilian city Sao Paulo, Paul Sergio Riedel uses his great-grandfather's name as his artist's name.

Since participating in his first exhibition in the city of Peruibe in 1972, his activities in the art scene are numerous and diverse.

No matter if he has been working as a painter, photographer, singer or dancer, Paul always dreamed of showing his skills in every artistic aspect.

Today, Paul Riedel lives in his second home Munich.

Preface

Prejudices have always been part of the human process of socialising. No matter which nation, what age or which race or religion, they will always be part of our society. Some are caused by overconfidence, others by envy or by another impetus.

Researchers, psychologists or sociologists explain this part of our behaviour as a protection mechanism, acting against strangers or the general environment. No matter how you look at it, be it a difference of age, gender or simply one's ancestry, prejudices are part of the human behaviour. Every day we have to fight our own biases, or these from others, so they do not hinder our development in society. Tolerance, as part of our natural resistance, became a rare resource in a word where cultures no longer meet over books.

Our society agrees that no one is willing to give a second chance when it comes to first impressions. This confirms the dominating mindset. However, not seldomly services and qualities of a person can only be seen at second glance. Sometimes, only then a person can be judged properly.

On social media, pro and contra arguments on mostly mundane topics clash. No matter if the post is about religion, animal treatment or fashion, one in two people are prone to insult or vilify their opposite. This behaviour is caused as a result of a stress response because of a flood of information. Furthermore, on social media, opinions are being manipulated by marketing agents which create numerous pseudo identities and claim to be part of local society.

I looked into the general characteristics of prejudices. Even though, a perfect and desirable personality free of any prejudices can be created on paper, the truth remains that our evolution is far from coming to an end.

Where rationality comes in to try and help us to see how senseless prejudices are, we agree. However, actually thinking about it is most of the time only the second action.

This book will tell about the background of the art market and its difficulties in the organisation of exhibitions. Many newcomers take it for granted for their first painting to do as well as the masterpieces of renowned artists. Most of the new starters think they will be discovered by showing their art at exhibitions. However, the market looks for experience and prominence, both of which are not easy to obtain and require a lot of work. Even the easy promise for a sales commission is not sufficient for the effort of trustees and art dealers, as the number of sold art pieces determines if a piece is just decoration or worth investing in.

During my research, I leaned on some of the experience my colleagues made. Thank you very much for all the time-consuming interviews. The experience which I share here was confirmed by several respondents during a lot of entertaining conversations. As an artist, I made a few of these experiences myself which now helps me to tell them.

This short novel is about the psychological aspects as well as the specific background of this scene and provides a unique insight for art lovers.

Midday

When Myrte arrived, the gallery was still closed to the public. The midday sun had a hard time shining through the ultra-violet filter of the windows, painting the gallery in a heavy, cool light. Pictures and statues were positioned perfectly beneath a heavy scent of unpacked card boxes. The walls were covered flawlessly in fresh white paint, and the light of the lamps shone perfectly onto the pieces of art. Next to every object was a description of the artist and the price the piece sells for.

Myrte was a slim, blonde woman in her late thirties. She already suffered from a few premature crow's feet. Too often Myrte had fleeting relationships, but she never let a man be part of her life. Emotions cause more stress which someone, as focused on their profession, does not need. She was of average build, and her looks suited the business she worked in. Although she was almost underweight, her blood pressure was slightly too high. On autumn days like these, this causes her a headache. Like so many in the business of art mediation, Myrte was self-employed and fought for her income with art projects. She was especially well known for her high selling numbers.

She looked at her work and was very satisfied. Every three months when she was ordered to be in the Bavarian town of Ludwigsstadt for the organisation of an exhibition, the gallery looked like this. She was already working in this sector for more than seven years and, although her organisation is perfect every time, she always felt like it is her first day of work. Every supplier had another concept, and every artist was a special case. Not forgetting every gallerist had a different business strategy. She only seldomly met Mr Benner, the owner of this art gallery.

The gallery was located close to the posh museum quarter in Munich and parking in the city centre was almost impossible. For this reason, Myrte did not have another chance but to take the public transport and to drag all her maps and her laptop around with her.

She did not see Mr Brenner very often, and his office was only open for four hours in the midday. He was said to be eccentric. In Munich, costs for businessmen always increased, and purchases were very hard to estimate, primarily because of the competition of the internet.

The following evening, they wanted to celebrate the 10th anniversary of the gallery and invited a lot of prominences. The artists they picked for this exhibition were, in Myrte's opinion, a lot of philistines but their art was cheap and probably easy to sell. Good artists are best off in museums and pinacothecas and accordingly very expensive. During the last four weeks, Myrte spent a lot of time in marketing and managed to increase the publicity of the gallery and of the project which she was leading.

The main problem she faced with these newcomers was that they, most of the time, tried to take over her role in discussing with potential clients and thus are stealing her provision. Meetings ending in exchanging business cards or looking for websites of artists became a hurdle for the artist themselves. For Myrte, they were no artist but businessmen who spend their free time creating art.

Spiritual paintings, experiences made during rehab or people who, after not succeeding in their profession, are looking for a new job and think a one-use art set can make them a name in the art scene. Those were the most common backgrounds of the artists at Myrtes exhibition. She had to decline others who already made themselves a name as a fortune teller, junkie or a case for social services. Before taking on a new artist, she had to spend a lot of time on the internet, looking for non-existent galleries or forgeries of honours or titles.

For Myrte, it was a wild mixture, but they could pay better than most of the invited guests. She called this concept "New Art Evolution", trying to bring a flair of New York into this scenario.

Investing in art survives on repeated mediation of already existing pieces and only seldomly on new art. But many do not understand this concept.

Myrtes strategy proved itself before, and she was sure she could hold a vernissage and come out of it with a slight plus in profit. After surviving this evening, she would treat herself to a break. She did not have a holiday in two years, and she could feel it. Sometimes, her back was in a lot of pain, and her nerves were shattered. You could say Myrtes mood shifted rather quickly these days.

She turned the lights on and admired her work again. She opened the door to get some refreshment, and the cool air flooded the room.

In Bavaria, the most significant art trade is limited to a very narrow circle. Only every now and then new artists are taken on, and vendors are mostly picked from the families of current members of this close group. Nevertheless, Myrte did not give up trying to get into these groups. However, as a woman with foreign roots, she did not think it would be very likely.

At this time, mostly the newly rich or tourists purchased art. No one had a particular background in art, nor did they value investing in art very much. Unfortunately, people who offer art for this kind of exhibition are only good amateurs. On the following evening, there were only two trained artists present and those who can pay the entrance fee, as well as an artist invited by the owner of the gallery.

Myrte was already bored of their go-to comments like "Maybe it is because I do not have a qualification in it …" etc. Once, she lost her temper and simply said to her potential art buyers that she hopes she does not apply for a job as a brain surgent with such an attitude. Primarily because of the eight years she already spent at university, she thought the trivialisation of education to be mainly negative.

She looked through her Blog where all the recent notifications in which she was involved were listed. Some Blogger had negative feedback regarding this project and called Myrte an exploiter of the poor artists. However, as Myrte already stated in a prior interview, artists had to prove themselves to gain the trust of agents and customers. Looking closer, she had to notice that these negative bloggers vainly tried to make themselves a name in the art industry themselves. Criticism like theirs was likely to be an attempt to create trustees and patrons, both of which Myrte saw as rather impossible.

In general, it is not possible that every offered art piece will find a new home and the costs had to be covered by someone. However, she was happy because her video talking about this topic had more views than the articles of these bloggers.

She turned the coffee machine in her office on, and the room was flooded with the noise of running engines grinding coffee beans.

Myrte checked the guest list and printed it out to place it on the desk at the entrance area. Next to every name, the name of their company and their profession was noted. This was important for her and her colleagues as these references show the possibility of the guest to buy an artwork. A star next to a name means this person made a purchase before and a moon indicates an abonnement of her catalogue. This catalogue of already mediated art pieces was positioned for anyone interested in it. Until now, she could always mediate an older piece again, which made the investment in art profitable for clients.

Art was sold for many different reasons. Sometimes, a buyer was not rich enough anymore and had to sell the art, or the owner died. There are a lot of reasons for a new profitable mediation for the vendor, resulting in a lucrative business for Myrte as well.

For the following evening, Myrte expected it to be busy; however she knew that her risky concept could go wrong as well. Still, Mr Brenner was very convinced of this idea.

He asked his assistant to set up the contracts and mentioned several times how much he liked her concept. Myrte had to pay special attention to mediating the art piece of a guest artist. In her opinion, this artist was more of a pseudo prominence. She called herself Honourable Sophie as if such title ever existed. Myrte was sure that the art piece was bought and in case the Honourable's name really was Sophie; it would not only be a surprise but a wonder.

Honourable was a lower title of nobility in the United Kingdom and its colonies. The art piece was a painting which, in Myrtes opinion, had too much orange paint on it. Other than orange colour, there were hints of carmine, sepia and anthracite. Most of the time this is a coincidence or a reasonable attempt to copy Francis Bacon's usage of a scraper. The painting was nothing unusual for Myrte, but she had to admit it was striking. Part of this distinctiveness of the artwork was the imagined meaning by the artist and the recommendation of the commissioner.

A hairy man knocked on the still-open door. Myrte went from the office into the cool room and saw the man at the door. His yellow T-shirt was not very flattering for his round stomach and left an undesirable gap where the hairy beginning of his stomach was visible. Black trousers combined with a clipboard let her assume it was a deliverer.

Myrte pushed the chair at the door out of the way.

"Can I help you?"

"I am here to deliver the glasses and bottles for the reception". Myrte secretively judged by his accent that this was the only phrase he knew in this language. For this reason, she held her index finger up and rotated it to her left side, where the catering kitchen will be arranged. She received a text message, which, on days like these, did not mean good news. The cabaret artist will be substituted by his teacher, who is a performance artist.

Just as the deliverer walks off into the direction of the kitchen, Theodor came to the door. Theodor belonged to the group of people that can be described in one word: Drama.

Under a mass of decorative cotton shawls, Theodor wanted to bring to mind that it was really hard for him and it was costly for him to get to this place. Furthermore, he stated that as an employee, he would not be affordable, however as a freelancer Myrte would get more than a good price. Myrte knew how to get her expectations across, and Theodor was very imaginative in implementing them. A cold wind accompanied him through the entrance door, and Myrte shivered.

Drama

"Theodor, what a busy bee you are." Three blown kisses sealed the foreplay. He was barely taller than 1,60 m, and his five-centimetre heels in the style of the 70s did not help in making him look taller. A green beret covered his right side of his small head and his dark hair was completely straight and brushed to the left. He liked to use this hat to claim his family is French, as the Italian roots of his family were not artistic enough for him. Underneath the shawls a half-opened jumper in moss green became visible, perfectly matching his dark tartan trousers which he bought in Scotland. Out of his over-sized bag he pulled a folder with the label "Brenner birthday exhibition".

"I had to work the whole evening yesterday, but the contracts are in order and checked now. Two attendees did not pay their entrance fee yet, and at least two will want their money back."

"What do you mean?"

"Dear poor people, canny savers and lawyers are not good customers, and you should know that by now. Wolfgang Hartmann is, with the work that he does, not even able to pay for the luxury he treats himself to and after the trouble he made to complete a transaction in the last second, I heard all the alarm bells go off in my head. Theodor waved his hand and the map in the other hand around to create a more dramatic effect.

"The woman I never remember the name of", after a short break he continued: "Does not matter. I saw her website, and she copies the African phase of Modigliani so shamelessly. We should definitely talk about plagiarism. So? The money withdrawal was declined and, although a friend of hers transferred us the money, she refuses to cover the bank charges. The account or the name of her account she listed was wrong. Very smart, right?" Myrte laughed and walked through the empty gallery to the office while the deliverer once again ran with his trolley into the door.

"She either pays at the entrance in cash or you shove her the abominableness pieces under her arm and abandon her." Myrte raised her voice: "I will hold you responsible for every damage on this door."

She did hear the following grumble of the deliverer but decided to ignore it.

In his obsequious position, Theodor followed her like a lapdog and showed the door to the deliverer, to make the complaint obvious.

"You did a good job with this exhibition." His head turned in every direction, and his not particular small nose nodded several times to show his approval.

"Oh, dear!" He put his free hand onto his chest as if he was in shock. With wide opened eyes, he moved his hand and pointed his finger at the five art pieces which were presented at the pedestals.

"Did she have to make five attempts to get the form of these right? I would have told her after the first one that she should not use clay." He laughed.

"The colour corrected pictures on your website are better than the grey original" Theodor looked at the other sculptures closely and shook his head.

"Yes, dear, this is the art of the woman who you were talking about. She was a programmer at a car company and does not only have money problems but also a shortage of talent. For this exhibition, however, I did not have another option as she contacted me for three years now. I could not decline her any longer."

Theodor read the sign next to the five clay statues.

"The five Masai? She must have used dildos as her template. Where are their arms or legs? We definitely have to keep this from the press." Unfortunately, Theodor's opinion was more accurate than Myrte wished for but also a signifier for the following evening.

"Looking at the size, I will definitely have to get to know this model." Ringing laughter followed Theodor's joke.

The delivery of glasses and beverages was successfully stored in the kitchen. Later on, the waitresses can work in there.

"I am done with the delivery. I left my business card at the counter for you. In case something is missing, or you want to order anything else, I will be in the office until 6 pm. See you."

Wow, Myrte thought, the Mediterranean looking deliverer is not only fluent, he also used the local dialect. She did not expect that. Although she grew up in Bavaria, she was never invited to the traditional clubs, and she never wore a Dirndl (the traditional Bavarian dress) outside of the largest folk festival, Oktoberfest.

The two assistants came already around the corner. They had to be briefed on the descriptions and explanations of the art pieces. Myrte walked them through the exhibition and handed out two tablets. On those tablets the descriptions of the artworks could be read off of the website as well.

"The video introduction on the website can be played by the guests on their smartphones as well. This saves a lot of work. All reservations can be entered via smartphones. Please have a look at these pages." Myrte tapped on her new devices.

Afternoon

Theodor was on his way to the laundry shop where he had to pick up his and Myrte's evening attire. No matter how clean rented clothes are, she always insisted on an extra wash and it paid off several times already.

The entrance desk was the favourite spot of Theodor. Guestlist and till stood there, ready for him to work on when he returned with his formal dressing. As agreed, the assistants were wearing white dresses.

"It's meeeee…!", shouted Theodor, to get someone's attention.

"I had to accept the performance artist last minute. Michel declined us suddenly. It seems he fell in love again", Myrte moans.

Michel was a trained historian and a good cabaret artist with a lot of charm. He presented most recent political decisions and compared these to historical events on alternative stages in the whole of Bavaria. Unfortunately, every crush he had in his life cost him the focus on his career.

"He gained more than ten kilos in the last twelve months, so his new crush has to be a restaurant owner or a fridge vendor." Theodor laughed louder than ever. This could also be down to the empty prosecco bottle he drank in the afternoon. For this reason, Myrte took his glass to put it into the dishwasher and looked at him rebuking.

"Last minute? You're boisterous. Where do you know this performance artist from?"

"I do not know her. Michel recommended her, and apparently she is his music artist and teaches at university", said Myrte disinterested. She was still looking at the confirmed press list.

"Lisa, could you please look after the guests from the press. Please do not let them talk to the artists. I do not want blunders or suffering artists who denounce us at the press. You can find the lists of press guests online."

"No Problemo." Lisa did not have a lot of experience, but she was always in a good mood and able to follow instructions.

"Dear, I am not a professional but to agree to a performance artist you never saw before seems risky. That is not very much like you. What was the reason?" Theodor was straightforward and always said what is on his mind.

"Honestly, I think I was just too tired, and that is why I will go on a forty-day long, well-deserved holiday after this exhibition. I already booked three Greek islands and paid a travel agent who knows all the hotels and cities, so I do not have to get stressed because I have to rely on the recommendations online. Michel only sent me a text message, which means that he is not in the mood for conversations."

Myrte was too tired already, and it was not easy to keep a business going and to fight off the competition. It is especially hard in Munich as the city and its art scene is very small. As they say, art is part of dramaturgy so everyone can claim to be an expert without having to prove it.

Only a few artists were trained in the sector, and those who were only seldomly had sponsors. That is why it got harder to make a living out of this. Actually, Myrte thought, it was never easy to make a living as an artist. For this reason, she became a curator and art dealer and never thought about becoming an artist herself.

"Lisa! After the performance artist is done, we will play some music in the background and let the computer try to soften up our guests for two hours. Please turn off the music fifteen minutes before the end. Let it fade out. Tactfully. Alright?" Myrte seemed to be a bit confused. Lisa nodded her head to show that she agreed.

The caterers were two brothers who always worked together. They weren't twins but had the same haircut and sense of style. Both had a similar figure which made it very easy to confuse them. As soon as they arrived, they were busy with preparations, similar to two synchronised swimmers.

Based on experience, finger food is gone within the first hour. After that, it will be down to only beverages and cleaning services. Even at the best events, it can never be avoided to have a few slightly tipsy guests. That is why the caterer organises the clearing of the tables and the cleaning afterwards.

Together with the caterers, the dressers arrived as well and a girl, maybe a bit too young for the job, dressed in uniform. She was hired to be a helping hand for the two brothers.

Theodor came out of the side room, which was now turned into a dressing room. He wore a tuxedo with extremely high shoulder pads. He almost looked like a character out of the nostalgic comic series "The Jetsons". In this series from the 60s, which is about the future of our society, everyone wore a futuristic suit. The authors believed this to be the trend in the future.

Inspiration

"One hour left, my dear. Where is your performance, artist? We should ask her about her plan and make sure it will not be too big of a surprise to us." On days like these, Theodor was a bit more stressed than he usually is. Secretly, he only wanted to see Michel again, but that is better kept private. He did not wait for a response as he knew he will not get one from Myrte anyways. He approached the door to roll out the carpet.

"Oh!", a soft voice whispered over the stooping Theodor.

"It is me who will be the first one on the red carpet?"

"And who exactly are you?" Theodor asked a bit tense.

"The artist for the opening performance", she said as if it was apparent.

"No, and you are definitely too late," Theodor replied harshly and pointed his finger in the direction of the dressing room. Delayed Melissa looked like she spent most of her salary already at the hairdresser. According to the glitter rag she was wearing, she was advised by a transvestite on her shopping day. Theodor judged it as old-fashioned. He was appalled at her being the replacement for charming Michel.

As soon as the red carpet was rolled out, Annegret Beyer stood there. She was a strictly looking woman in her late forties, dressed in traditional black clothes. She stood, with an even stricter look on her face, at the end of the red carpet. Amongst other things, she was the one who created the Masai-group.

"We are not open yet."

"That was not my question," Annegret stated harshly.

"Good." Theodor was visibly affected by her teasing. "That makes me a fortune teller, and I looked into the future where you would ask me this question. I can also see that you will return in one hour." He made a dramatic pause and turned around on his heel and said: "See you." He was always ready to fight and had the perfect tone of voice for customers like these.

"You are quite unfriendly."

Theodor closed the door behind him. However, Annegret was not in a good temper either and followed him through the door.

"Do you want me to call the police and issue a ban on entering the house or are you ready to leave voluntarily?

Myrte witnessed the aggressive vibe in the room and tried to calm it down immediately. She thinks that sometimes, Theodor's bravery can damage her business.

"What is the problem here? We are not open yet.", she explained.

"Your employee extorted me for money. That is the problem." Annegret lifted her chin one centimetre up to emphasise her pride.

"Dear, please, not now. The contract states clearly that the payment is in advance, and he only did what I asked him to. He did not want to be personal. Please, could you come back in one hour? I am sure you will like our work."

Annegret felt patronised, but she realised everyone was stressed and her complaints were at the wrong place here. She saw the Masai group on its five pedestals on the other side of the room. She had to admit they look much better presented like this than she remembered them to look like.

The performance artist hummed and danced around. With her hands, she painted not very elegant lines in the air. She counted her steps and repeated some.

Theodor went back to his work and left Myrte and Annegret alone. He was not convinced by the dancing Melissa. She was old and, although she probably looked good in her younger years, he thought she might be a bit overwhelmed by the upcoming performance.

"I still see the value of my art to be much higher than you estimated, and I came by to clarify this", argued Annegret.

"Dear." Myrte used this word, so she does not have to remember the names of everyone she talks to. It got a lot worse in the last twelve months. "You are unknown, and your work is not original enough for the price you imagine. That is why I stated in the contract for how much I will try to offer your work. With a moderate hourly rate, this price is more than fair." Theodor stood behind Annegret and tried to signalise the question if he should start packing the Masai group up. Myrte raised her hand for a second.

"The contract was a mistake. I am aware of that. I just try to protect myself of more damage. Especially the comments on your website were very positive, and I am sure one of them will be interested in buying these art pieces."

However, Annegret knew that most of the comments were written by marketing agents and the only people commenting were her and one of her friends.

"Two, three and step", someone whispered behind the group. Theodor looked at Melissa angrily and made it evident that she is at the wrong place right now. Melissa, visibly offended, walked with her chin up in the direction of the dressing room.

"Seriously Dear, I do not have time. Just take your pieces with you and a cancellation fee will be everything you have to pay. Now decide. Theodor will be happy to pack everything for you to take it with you. Alright?" It was not a question but an obvious hint that the conversation came to an end. All of Annegret's pride went away and was replaced by truculence.

"So?" challenged Theodor.

"I can live with this damage, but you will never play tricks on me like this again."

"I want you to give me the transfer fees as well. In cash and right now."

They discussed all formalities and continued the preparations. But not Melissa. She sat in the dressing room and fought with her nerves. She took off her glittery dress and revealed a skin-tight, black bodysuit. She wanted it to be neutral so she could attach the details for her dance on it. It was a challenge for her, and she wanted to show that age is not everything defining her. Some years ago, Melissa knows that she delighted a lot of people and especially men.

She looked in the mirror she brought with her and started preparing her face for the makeover. Maybe she bit off more than she could chew, but she was convinced she will shine tonight. A lot of emotions came up, and she almost started crying. All those people belonged to a younger generation and did not like her, but she really needed the money and wanted to feel alive during her performance. The base of her makeup was already applied. She combined a see-through scarf with her black bodysuit, which she picked especially for tonight. The last time she wore it was her course graduation. Melissa herself created the dance of the praying mantis and thought its strongest point was its originality. She took a deep breath in and looked around the room for one last time. She walked past Theodor who did not even look at her. Yes, she had everything she needed for this short performance, but afterwards she wanted to leave as soon as possible. She could not handle more resentment.

As expected, Theodor opened the door at 7 p.m., but no guests were there yet. The weather was wet and slightly windy. Not very inviting to leave the house but it was still better than the warm nights where Myrte had to compete with all the other events in the city.

The performance was scheduled to start at 8 p.m. so most guests would probably arrive at about 7:30 p.m. The last-minute change of the programme was written on a chalkboard, as well as online on their website. They were never sure if Michel turned up, so Myrte never mentioned him in the programme. Now, it turned out this was a smart move.

Nancy Wilson, a Jazz artist, was played in the background, and the room was filled with yellow daylight. Spots of bright white light were directed to shine on to the paintings and sculptures. The first guests approached the door and the evening took its course.

First up was a woman with a pram.

"Good evening and welcome to the anniversary of Brenner's gallery!" Theodor was charming and very professional. His hair was backcombed a bit too much, which made it look very artistic. "Because of safety and liability reasons, could I please ask you to leave the pram at the cloakroom."

The woman was shocked. "You mean I have to carry my child around for the whole night?" She pushed the pram further and scraped some of the varnish off the wall.

Theodor smiled and did not reply but stood in a position so the woman could only go into the direction of the cloakroom. Prams are, after empty glasses, the biggest risk in exhibitions. Although Theodor liked children, he had to ask himself if art exhibitions are the right place to bring them. In the middle of his thoughts he was interrupted by new guests.

The girl at the cloakroom took on the job as a babysitter. Theodor was busy welcoming the new guests and did not care about the small extra bonus the girl received for her babysitter service.

Myrte tried to calm herself down in the backroom. As Theodor noticed, she was not in the best mental state, and the situation did not get better after Annegret started crying.

The young woman at the cloakroom handed out, pick up slips and put down the clothes she got handed over very neatly. The poor baby slept in its pram and did not notice the exchange of clothing. The guests were supposed to pay for their drinks. The times of free beverages in galleries did only result in a lot of drunk people who never even bought a postcard. That is why Myrte handled her exhibitions like a visit to the theatre where no one gets free drinks. The most significant advantage was that there were less drunken people who then cause damage to the interior of the gallery.

"It is improbable that I have to pay for my own beverages during an exhibition", said a snippy woman into the direction of Theodor.

"In case you will buy one of the art pieces, I will be happy to pay you back the amount of money you spent on drinks myself." He smiled, and the woman understood and smiled back.

A tall woman in a blue dress made out of Thai silk approached the entrance. Her long, red hair was typical for an Irish woman. She put up her hair to an awe-inspiring art piece which partly covered her face as well. Theodor thought Sophie is a bit too tall for a woman and looked at her feet. He was impressed by the designer shoes and especially their size. Shoes that size were not cheap and most of the time handmade. He was proud of his small feet and thought he could probably walk better in those stilettos than Sophie.

"Honourable Sophie", he whispered her name.

Theodor found the name on the list of the artists and wanted to say something nice as a greeting.

"Sophie, welcome."

"Honourable Sophie, please." Theodor coquetted his hand on his chest and replied with an agreeing "Ohh". Both of them put on a dishonest simile no one would believe, and she entered the room.

The room was crowded, and almost everyone from the press was there as well. Honourable Sophie covered her face as Ralf, the photographer, approached. She showed him that she would rather not be in the spotlight. She wore long, fake fingernails painted in a dark blue. They helped to make her slightly big hands look a bit smaller.

Only seldomly all reporters on the list actually showed up, and they always got free beverages. There were already more spontaneous visitors than usually, and Theodor hoped some of them would leave soon. With so many visitors, it is hard to actually have conversations. He handed the job of controlling the entrance to one of the brothers of the catering and tried to get in contact with the guests. There were sixteen artists in the room which cost a lot of space. Theodor did not want them to be at the actual exhibition, but sometimes they bring new guests with them.

It was drizzling, and Theodor's hair suffered under the humidity.

Myrte stepped out of the dressing room where she watched Melissa while she put on her makeup. Secretly, she hoped that she will not have to put as much makeup on as her when she was sixty years old. Melissa's wrinkly skin was full of facial powder and shimmered slightly green.

Myrte herself looked amazing. She tried to create a contrast to the art pieces with her moss-green dress. She wore elegant stilettos with a metal embellishment in the form of a leaf. She put her hair up with hair lacquer, and she looked like just another artwork in her gallery.

The voice of Dean Martin was followed by a silent piano. Lisa focused on dimming the main lights a bit. Theodor realised this sign and walked in the middle of the room where he rang a little bell to get the attention of all guests.

Melissa opened the door of the dressing room a bit to listen if it was her turn already. She realised it was too early for her to come out, so she closed the door again slightly too loudly. This noise confused Myrte, and she kept looking at tonight's guests.

"Dear Ladies and Gentlemen, welcome at the Brenner gallery." A dramatic pause signalised some guests did still not pay attention.

Theodor walked up to Myrte, and finally the room became silent.

"Today, for the anniversary of this gallery, we present 50 art pieces, each of them created by new artists. I will guide you through the gallery myself and will tell you about the pieces. Our team of photographers will capture a few moments tonight. In case someone does not want to be in the spotlight of the camera, please talk to Ralph directly", Myrte laughed because of her own joke and Ralph joined in. The guests applauded quietly.

Dance

"The evening will start off with Melissa's performance, followed by my tour through the gallery. I hope you will enjoy Melissa with her dance of the praying mantis."

Theodor, who was still unsure about Melissa's performance, signalised Lisa to turn on the song the artist wished for. Theodor recognised the song after the first few seconds. Her choice was not the best for an occasion like tonight. Melissa picked the Bolero by Ravel, a song which is used for performances a little too often nowadays. It was the song of the advertisements for ice cream and tampons which did not make the best impression for an energetic performance. Theodor became slightly nervous when Melissa did not show up after the song was already playing for sixteen seconds. He walked to the dressing room and opened the door. He caught Melissa by surprise, and she quickly stopped smoking the cigarette which she took from the security guard. She was so shocked, she started coughing immediately. Those disturbing noises annoyed Myrte slightly more than usual. She seemed cold and angry.

Theodor went back to the computer and played the song from the beginning. His scepticism slowly turned into anger. The music started again, and Melissa came out of the dressing room dressed in black leggings and a purple scarf made out of silk. She managed to just barely lift up a leg and took a step towards her left in the direction of the entrance door. Her missing flexibility revealed her age, but it was noticeable she was passionate about this performance. Lisa closed the door behind Melissa and Ralph turned on his photographer mode, taking picture after picture. Melissa attached two peacock feathers onto her headband. It looked exotic; however, Theodor did still not seem convinced. Myrte looked more surprised than expected.

Melissa acted and danced like an insect. She approached the first art piece, and horrible noises came out of her throat. Everyone who knows famous Japanese horror films would be reminded of "Mothra" by Ishiro Hinda. Melissa now even sounded like an insect.

This was the moment Myrte realised what Melissa meant when she said she will sing to the art pieces. Starting of weird and scurrile, the show turned into a grotesque interpretation of a Kabuki theatre. Its Japanese roots were evident for everyone, even if someone did not know anything about it. With not more than a minute into the performance, Myrte felt like an hour had passed already and she could not wait until it was over. Theodor could sense her tense emotions.

Melissa danced dangerously close to the art pieces, and the feathers on her head moved up and down in the rhythm to the demonic dance or however, this performance could be described. Theodor was in charge of the music and knew that the following four minutes of this dance could ruin the whole evening. He turned up the pace of the music. Fortunately, Bolero can be played slightly faster, without people noticing it negatively. Melissa stuck to the rhythm of the music, and the feathers on her head did as well. She already reached the Masai group when Melissa, who acted like she was possessed by the ghost of Isadora Duncan, performed her apotheosis. She whirled around, and you could see that she, despite some stiff body parts, gave everything for this performance. A lot of different sounds came out of her throat which should describe the various art pieces. Although this was quite an original idea it did not prove very fruitful.

Theodor could not wait until the last twenty seconds were over. The unsettled guests already started giving their half-empty champagne glasses back. He thought this could not be a good sign.

With ten seconds until the end, Melissa came to perform her big finale. Her head spun around itself. Theodor had to think of "The Exorcist" by Linda Blair and had to smile. One of the feathers snapped on the hanging lamp and Melissa was so surprised, the other feather caught in one of the Masai figures and pulled it to the ground.

The room was tranquil. Shock and quiet laughter followed and after the music was over everyone was still. Myrte turned red and not even the lighting in the room could hide it. Theodor sensed that something horrible will happen, probably even worse than the performance they just witnessed.

Lisa turned the lights back on.

Melissa finished her dance and ended in a bow. She rushed towards the dressing room, knowing that an encore would not be necessary.

"You ruined my Masai group!", shouted Annegret.

Theodor waved at Eivan, the security guy. He took Annegret's arm nicely but determined and asked her to come with him into the side room. Meanwhile, one of the caterers picked up the pieces of the shattered Masai statue.

"Art is temporary. Art is unusual. Art is real life. Our task is …", Myrte tried to save the situation. The colour of her face was slightly less red, but you could still see the anger in her eyes. "Suffering and overcoming, looking for perfection. Thank you, Melissa, for this interpretation. Please, dear guests, follow me around and I will show you the other art pieces. "

The art of distraction is magical. There never was a moment where this saying was as appropriate as now.

"You do not smoke in an art gallery, stupid!", Theodor was bright red which did not happen very often.

"I was nervous, as an artist, this is …" She could not finish the sentence before she started crying again.

"Oh, shut up and leave."

"You did not pay me yet", sniffed Melissa.

"And you will wait until we get the invoice for the broken statue. I will see you tomorrow. Now, leave. You did enough for tonight and do not dare talk to the guests about this performance." Theodor left the dressing room and tried to regain his composure. In all those years he worked together with Myrte, this was the first time so many things went wrong.

Roosemary Clooney played in the background. Lisa and Anne handed out catalogues and typed addresses for the website in their phones.

Obviously, the whole room was talking about the praying mantis. The performance left the guests with a mixture of persiflage and modern art. Some were laughing out loud, and others were looking for its academic and scientific explanation. Not enough people understood the reference to modern Japanese culture.

"Modern art is just something controversial. Melissa is your name, right?", asked the Honourable Sophie in a light baritone voice in the middle of the group of guests she was talking to. She did not wait for Melissa to reply but just continued herself: "She just dropped all classical conventions and created her own expressions based on the modern Japanese culture, I guess. Not many would find the courage to do so, am I right?" Sophie waited for her opinion to sink in. One of the reporters seemed like he could understand what the Honourable Sophie just said.

All men were very fond of her intellectual opinions. Theodor was not quite sure why Sophie triggered some kind of discomfort in him.

Myrte was busy with a few potential customers. Eivan talked to Annegret, and you could barely hear the music in the background because of the noise of all the conversations. It was evident that, no matter how high the quality of Melissa's performance was, it definitely made the night unforgettable.

Lisa and Anne marked the first paintings as reserved and noted all details of the buyers in their online contracts.

The Masai group did still grieve about its lost friend. Myrte tried to conceal her anger with other conversations.

"These pieces of art were created to remind us of our origin in Africa. Parts of the profit of these pieces will go to the African fund, which supports the development of education in villages in Nigeria." She did not tell lies, just selected the right words. The truth was that Annegret herself was the chairman of this association which receives donations like these.

"Will these pieces be in your catalogue once they are mediated again?", asked a woman in the group pointing her finger at the remaining Masai.

"Although it is not the plan yet, I would not say no." She could not disguise the truth completely. These statues were horrific, and the possibility of this artist creating any better work soon is seen as very unlikely by Myrte's regular customers. Myrte realised the background of this question and wanted to give an explanation for this future prognosis as the conversation was interrupted by an outraged Annegret.

"I can recreate the broken piece. I am sure the connection which I have to my past will always be present inside of me." You could read in Myrte's face what she thought of this appearance. It was graceful but not wished for.

"Have you lived in Africa?", asked the same woman who just asked Myrte about her catalogue. According to her looks, she would not buy this piece, but she could create a reason for others to be interested in it.

"Yes", replied Annegret. Myrte was not very sure about this as she did not know her very well, but she was sure Annegret never mentioned travelling to Africa before. She was chairman of an association which sends donations to Africa. Annegret was happy about this gained attention and continued:

"Once, a shaman explained to me during my own shaman training that in an earlier life, I lived in Africa." She had a spiritual expression in her face and tried to sound modest.

"Wow. A spiritual experience. How unlikely", commented the unknown woman.

"Ha. Hum. Well, I did not know that myself. You should have told me this story as I am always very interested in the background of the artists exhibiting at my gallery." Secretly, Myrte waved at Theodor who looked at a tall, blonde man in his fifties and lost a bit of his professionality.

"Yes. It changed my life. Never before would I have believed stories like these." An emphasising hand movement should lend weight to what she said. Myrte waved even more now and spilt a bit of her champagne.

Myrte could not hear anything anymore, and she felt dizzy. There were too many surprises for one evening, and now a shaman treated the professionality of this exhibition with contempt. Theodor seemed a bit tipsy, but he realised Myrte was not feeling well and hurried towards her.

"He trained me in the art of the shamanism, and I left my IT career for it. This sector was too negative for me and blocked the connections to my origin." Myrte almost started crying when a tall, black man with a handsome face approached the group. Myrte was close to screaming and apologising to the group.

"Probably, the broken piece took away the negative vibes which bordered you."

"Burdened", corrected Annegret.

"You seem very happy, ma cher."

"Oh well, it was the shaman", said Myrte without questioning it. Theodor understood the situation, held Myrte's hand and tried to calm her down.

"I am just telling them about how we met." Annegret kissed the man lightly on his cheek, and everyone immediately understood their relationship. The group looked at each other, and some seemed a bit jealous as the shaman was so charming.

Theodor did not want to snub the group and left with Myrte after Annegret stole all the attention from her.

"What kind of people are they?", complained Myrte.

"We never asked these people much about their lives. Surprises like these were not unlikely."

"At least the Honourable Sophie helped us out. She came up with such a good explanation for Melissa's performance. Enviable." Myrte shivered and tried to smile.

Anne and Eivan looked worried and walked towards Myrte. Eivan was a great security guy. Unfortunately, because of his law degree, he will no longer be able to work for her in two years.

Everyone had a good time. Lisa and Theodor were working hard and used Melissa's attention for themselves.

"It happened. We caught Mr Hartmann twice handing out his business cards after offering one of Anne's potential buyers to sell an art piece for a better price to them after this exhibition." Eivan waited for a response while Anne showed the already prepared warning statement.

Myrte had to learn during her time in this business how to act strict and professional. Many people underestimate her determination. But never again afterwards.

"Mark the painting with a black dot and bring him to me in the back room." Myrte was like a general on her own, perfectly well-known battlefield.

She put the statement down on the table in the backroom and only shortly after, Anne and Eivan arrived together with Wolfgang Hartmann.

"You know what this is about, right?", she asked him directly.

"How about 'Good afternoon'? You did not even say hello to me, nor did you honour my work." Myrte pointed her index finger upright in front of his nose. This seemed to work. It made Wolfgang jump, and he became silent.

"Now shut up. According to our contract, you will be banned from this exhibition immediately, and we will send you an invoice with the fee you will have to pay. Witnesses and proof are right here, and I do not have time for a discussion." Every potential interruption she just rejected with a hand movement.

Eivan came closer and took the warning statement and put it in an envelope.

"Mr Hartmann, as a witness and commissioner, I will now hand you this written document and ask you to follow me without attracting any kind of attention. Please mind our agreement on reputational damage." In the agreement, Eivan formulated everything correctly so artists could be fined because of typical scandals and emotional outbursts. He was sure, the harshly expressed words in the contract, as well as the cold speech Myrte gave Mr Hartmann had an impact on him.

Myrte already left the room, and Wolfgang tried to argue to prove his innocence, but he knew, the person in front of him did not have any interest in his argumentations.

Wolfgang left the room with his letter in his hand and Anne went into the exhibition room. Immediately, she put a black stripe on the sign of the painting. While she did that, she called the web exhibition and only one klick later, Wolfgang Hartmann was an irrelevant and forgotten story of this evening, as well as in Myrte's life.

Eivan watched Wolfgang Hartmann silently while he picked up his jacked under loud protest.

At the door, Eivan said to him strictly:

"We will send you the painting tomorrow. In the name of the house of Mr Brenner, I herewith issue a house ban for you."

Another artist, who watched the situation closely from another window, put her business cards into her wallet and tried to look away. She did not want to return Wolfgang's look.

"We came well prepared. It is a shame because of him. His picture is not even that bad, is it?" Anne commented.

"Well, who wants to swim with sharks has to prove a bit more skill. It is easy to alienate with Myrte, but it is also dangerous." Eivan closed the door and started looking at the hallway again.

When Eivan saw Theodor's face, he said: "Well, very smart." Both of them laughed about the incident which they already predicted before tonight.

Wolfgang stood in front of the gallery, feeling very upset. He stood there almost thirty minutes until his head became wet. He looked for a way to pay revenge to Myrte, but he soon realised there is no point. No one of the other artists seemed to care about Wolfgang, and when he left, no one even realised.

Ralph kept on taking pictures and avoided Honourable Sophie as much as possible. Myrte looked for something to distract her as she had a headache. She could not use any more drama after what just happened with Wolfgang. Theodor brought her back to reality.

"Only one hour left until we are done for today. We have a few inquiries from your catalogue." Theodor was quiet for a minute and looked at Myrte coquettish. "I have an appointment for a personal consultation with one of the buyers." He nodded into the direction of the blonde man who waved back to him.

"You too, Brutus?", said Myrte on the verge of despair.

"Do not go crazy. He is nice and the evening is alright. Annegret seems to have more fun than she initially expected. I offered Montolu, the shaman, money for the broken statue and we will invoice it with our insurance."

"Montolu?"

"It is his African name, but you can call him Frank as well."

"Slut." Myrte laughed and seemed to gain back her countenance. She went back to the crowd.

She did not believe anything could save this evening and saw how Melissa talked to one of the reporters. She felt a lump in her throat. She was convinced, Theodor said goodbye to her already, but apparently, she was mistaken.

Melissa stood next to the Honourable Sophie and explained her performance. She swung her arms up in the air and Ralph took pictures of her.

"At the moment I was invited to perform here, I was delirious with joy. An exhibition from Myrte." Melissa surely knew everyone could hear her, especially Myrte. She added in an even more arty way: "Especially at an anniversary like this. What an honour!" Apparently, Melissa tried to cover up her mistake to gain some popularity by kissing up to Myrte.

"Melissa", shouted Myrte surprised.

"The Honourable Sophie explained to me how extraordinary this performance was and asked me to write a critique for our newspaper. I am not familiar with the modern Japanese culture, but I would be very interested in an explanation", explained the reporter kindly.

Myrte felt dizzy and in the mood to start crying immediately. Negative critiques could ruin her future.

"Amazing. The performance was a pleasant, positive surprise for me as well", Myrte lied.

"Especially the connection between the movements and the art pieces led to a lot of people thinking about the meaning of them", added the reporter.

"It was a mixture of fury and grace in a unique female combination. Only a true artist can offer something beautiful as that. I can only say: Bravo, my dear Myrte!", said the Honourable Sophie in a slightly deeper baritone sound. Apparently, she already tried everything of the drink menu, but she definitely knew how to turn this catastrophe into an art miracle.

Melissa bowed down. The feathers on her head were no longer visible, and her bloodshot eyes glared a bit.

"I teach at the university. I teach lessons in art." Melissa's modesty disappeared slightly.

Myrte remembered the orange picture. It is still here, and she needs to sell it. Theodor came up to her and tried to understand what was happening.

The woman with the pram tried to get her coat back from the cloakroom. She seemed to have trouble standing up properly.

The caterer did a great job collecting all the empty glasses, and both assistants seemed busy as well. Myrte felt nervous. She just wanted the last hour to be over.

Michel, who cancelled his performance for tonight, came into the room accompanied by an older man. Their heads were shining from the water running down their faces. The cold and wet air was typical for this season, and they closed the door behind them very quickly. Michel looked neat and pleased with his life.

"Have you had sex, dear?" Theodor was straightforward and intimate; however they were good friends, and apparently his question was not very far from the truth. Theodor kissed the air, and Michel laughed guiltily.

"How was the performance of my teacher?"

"Refreshing." This already indicated more than Michel wanted to know.

"Seriously? Was it that bad?"

"We will see. She is talking to one of the critics and Myrte seems to be close to fainting."

"I wanted to come earlier, but we were invited to his parents. It is his father's birthday. I had to cancel on you."

Eivan, the security guy, tried to take a champagne glass from a woman who obviously did not take her sixth glass very well. She laughed loudly and weaved a bit. Theodor noticed this situation and wanted to end this greeting as soon as possible.

"Of course, Michel. We assumed something like this." Theodor could say something like this without turning red. He found very nicewords for it. "Go and mingle with the people. I am sure it will be a long night."

Eivan helped the drunk woman to get her coat and led her outside carefully.

Melissa was back in the room and thanks to the complimenting words of the Honourable Sophie, she gained more attention from the press. She now found herself in a group of admirers. Myrte was not sure about this situation, but she was thankful for this unexpected support.

Myrte wanted to try and sell the picture of the Honourable Sophie now. This was a big problem for her, as she did not know this woman, nor did she know anything about the background of this picture. Still, the Honourable Sophie was a massive help on this catastrophic evening. No one stood in front of this picture, and some guests even left after looking at it. She already resigned to not selling this picture tonight until she saw a red dot on the sign next to it.

"Lisa!", shouted Myrte.

"Who bought this painting?"

"An anonymous buyer bought it about twenty minutes ago via our auction portal."

On this online portal, Myrte recorded videos of herself commenting on different paintings. Visitors could register or buy art pieces without stating their identity. Myrte felt relieved and thought that there might be a god somewhere who actually liked her.

The Masai group stood still behind Annegret. She was busy saying healing prayers, including great hand gestures for an excited listener.

Myrte wanted to avoid this exhibition turning into an esoteric fair, so she hurried up to Annegret.

"I can see everyone is having a good time here", she greeted the group.

"Montolu, isn't it? I struggle with foreign names." Laughed Myrte and thought about her own name.

"Frank is sufficient; actually my name is Francis. Montolu is my African name." This was too much information for Myrte, who definitely learned enough tonight already.

"Apparently, the night was successful. I am very sorry because of the broken statue."

"No, please." Frank lifted his hand and had a stunning smile on his face.

"Can we please take these statues out of the exhibition? I will cover the cancellation fees", he asked.

"Why? This exhibition will still go on for six days." Myrte was slightly confused by this proposal.

"I want Annegret to bring these statues into our practice. It was a dispensation of god that one of them broke. Now, all four of them fit in there."

For a moment, Myrte did not know what to say when Theodor and his friend joined the group.

"I just told Kurt, there has to be a sign in this coincidence. We just did not see it in the beginning."

Myrte did not find any words and was glad that Monolu brought it up.

"Sure", she mumbled slightly unsure about this situation.

"Lisa, could you please mark this Masai group as Frank's?" Theodor took over this situation.

Myrte looked at her watch and was happy to see that she could leave this madhouse soon.

"Dear Ladies and Gentlemen, the evening will come to an end soon with only fifteen minutes until we close. Thank you very much for coming. For the next six days, we will still be open for you to visit this gallery."

There was more drama at the exit. The woman with the pram forgot her child at the cloakroom. Eivan laughed and tried to calm down the couple. Everyone else who saw what happened joined in the laughing.

The music of Marla Glen came to an end, a signal for the guests to finish up their drinks.

At the cloakroom the stressed girl returned faux furs, fancy second-hand coats and typical Bavarian jackets to their owners. The piggy bank seemed exceptionally fortunate on this generous evening.

"It was a fabulous but extraordinary evening", said the reporter.

"We are known for surprises, aren't we?" Theodor finished the sentence with a happy smile. Although he interrupted every conversation, Myrte was grateful for him to be there. Myrte herself could not take any more.

"I will honour your efforts in our paper on the weekend."

"I hope we will stay in contact." The Honourable Sophie joined the conversation.

Only when the reporter came closer for a goodbye kiss, she took one step back and smiled.

"I do not want your wife to find herself in a confusing situation", she said, offering her hand with a coquette smile. He fleetly kissed her hand and said his goodbyes.

While the reporter went into the direction of the cloakroom the Honourable Sophie went back to the bar and Myrte and Theodor were left alone. Both did not know what to say for a moment.

"What should I say? This woman saved our evening", noted Myrte.

"I am not too sure. Looking back on it, I feel guilty for this incident."

"Why?"

"I panicked and turned the pace of the song up for Melissa's performance to end sooner. I found her performance to be embarrassing. I do not know anything about Japanese art, and everything was a bit too original for me."

Myrte thought about this for a second. She could see why someone would treat this as an act of sabotaging the performance.

"It was not fair of you."

"No, I agree. I underestimated her, and I gave free rein to my prejudices."

For the first time tonight, Theodor admitted to himself that he made a mistake. He only saw her age and how she looked like but overlooked her good qualities. Her voice might not be as rich as the voice of a younger woman, and her steps might not be as graceful anymore, but she still is an artist at heart.

The other reporters in the room were jealous of the one reporter who already said goodbye to the Honourable Sophie. Apparently, he was Sophie's favourite. Now he was gone, and all of them were around Melissa who bowed down gracefully. With the help of Theodor, she answered countless questions and was grateful for all the lovely comments regarding her performance.

Myrte said goodbye to a few guests and did not forget about the nice comments for Melissa's new-found talent.

"I just wanted to make sure that we will get all four of the statues back. Is this correct?" Annegret and Frank came over from the cloakroom to say their goodbyes.

"Sure, and again, my apologies for this horrific accident. As far as I know, it was caused by the music which was not regulated correctly. However, everything is just fine. Frank, what an honour to get to know you. By the way, what kind of clinic do you own?"

"We are working with love." Frank looked at Annegret happily.

"There are couples who are looking for tantras or other alternatives to enhance their relationships. Most of the time, this ends in an embarrassing situation from which they will never recover in their lives. We developed our own technique. Here,
my business card." Frank's slightly French accent was tantalising and very charming.

Myrte took his business card and realised why Annegret was as uptight. She also noted that they maybe should talk about love in the near future.

Da capo

Everyone left, and the bar was ready to be picked up again. Anne and Lisa turned off the light spots, and only the sparse main light lit up the room. The sweet scent of fermented champagne, cleaning agents and sweat was in the air. Mixed with many perfumes, the air in this room needed changing. Anne opened the door widely and let fresh air come in.

The deliverer with the gap in his shirt, which made his stomach peak out parked on the pavement and the brothers loaded his car with inventory and rubbish. Because of the quick cleaning process, everything looked very hectic for Myrte. However, she did not mind it.

The last guest to be in the room was the Honourable Sophie. Melissa went with Michel and his new lover up the street and laughed full of joy. Apparently, she reached her goal.

"We did not have the opportunity to introduce ourselves", said Myrte politely.

"Unfortunately, it is quite late already, but I am sure we will see each other again."

Myrte did not expect this response. Sophie acted very reservedly. A behaviour which went well with the amount of makeup she had on her face. Myrte knew she was very familiar to Sophie's face, but she could not recall from where.

Sophie, who got her scarf back from the cloakroom, waved goodbye. As she went through the door, her scarf tangled slightly in flower in her hair. When she tried to pull it down again, her whole hair fell down as well. It was only a wig.

Suddenly, Myrte remembered that Mr Brenner did not attend the exhibition himself. But now she understood that his alter ego, the Honourable Sophie, represented him perfectly.

Further publications of this author

German novels
- Altreia, Drama, 1998
- Geheimnis der verdorrten Rosen, Mystery, 2009 – Reimo Verlag *
- Virtuelle Liebe, Kurzroman, Thriller, 2016 *
- Paloma, Kurzroman, Thriller, 2016 *
- Die Muse, Kurzroman, Erzählung, 2016 *
- Post Mortem Kino, Roman, Drama, 2016 *
- Die Heilerin, Roman, Thriller, 2017 *
- Geheimnis der verdorrten Rosen, Mystery, 2017 (neue Version) *
- Der Zauberspiegel des Eros, Roman, Thriller, 2017 *
- Das Tal, Roman, Thriller, 2017 *
- Jahreszeiten der Sünde, Roman, Thriller,2018*

English novels
- Virtual Affairs, 2018 *

German audio books
- Paloma, 2018
- Virtuelle Liebe, 2018

Art catalogues
- Geliebter Vater, 1995 *
- The new Artist, 1996 und 1997
- Liebe in Stücken, 2009 *
- Kunstkatalog, 2010
- Liebe in Stücken, Edition II, 2016 *
- Kunstkatalog, 2017 *
- Kunstkatalog, 2018 *
- Kunstkatalog, 2019 *

(*) Listed in the German National Library